We all know that Tooth Fairy works at night.
So probably she sleeps during daytime.
But how does she keep
everything done?

She has the best assistants ever!
Fairy Cook and Fairy Dentist.
Let's get to know them better.

"Hi, Sugar!" Fairy Cook welcomed her beloved Tooth Fairy home after a long night's work. She continued, "It's almost midday. You should get some sleep. I'm almost done here with our standard menu:

twenty chocolate cakes with strawberries on top, fifteen banana-caramel cakes, and fifteen rainbow cakes with chocolate glaze. Want to try one?"

When they entered the kitchen Tooth Fairy looked at the gorgeous cakes and exclaimed, "They are perfect! But we are still missing one ingredient, aren't we?" She winked and took a bag of magic powder out of her pocket.

"It was a brilliant idea to add your magic to my cakes," said Fairy Cook.

"Some children need cake that will help their tooth fall out fast. Not only a coin under the pillow," said Tooth Fairy with a smile.

"I love those sweet-teeth!" said Fairy Cook.

The same moment that the kitchen door opened, Fairy Dentist appeared. "Who said sweet-teeth?" she asked, looking strict. "Fairy Cook, I hope you remember how dangerous sugar is for your teeth."

"My dear aunty," said Tooth Fairy, "we always put your tooth-brushing instructions into the cake boxes. Don't worry! I am the Tooth Fairy. I want to collect healthy teeth."

Suddenly, Tooth Fairy remembered why she had decided to visit the kitchen before sleep. A girl called Alice feared losing her tooth so much that she had stopped eating. She was afraid that it would hurt when she took a bite.

"If we don't hurry up, Cookie, tomorrow Alice's mom will take her to the dentist." Tooth Fairy said.

"Dentist?' cried Fairy Cook. "No way!"

"What's wrong with a dentist visit?" asked Fairy Dentist.

"Oh ... that smell - those instruments!" Cookie made a face.

Fairy Dentist was outraged. She never understood those fears. Dentist pastes smelled like chewing gums and candies. They showed cartoons to kids and gave them little presents. Kids should love those dentist visits!

Tooth Fairy said, "You are right, Aunty! There's nothing wrong with a dentist visit. But it can spoil the magic of the first Loose Tooth. Cookie, please, do your best!"

Cookie said, "You go to bed, Fairy! I'll cook such a cake that all of Alice's fears will melt like chocolate!"

"Let the magic begin!" solemnly pronounced Tooth Fairy and went to bed.

Fairy Cook took out the yummiest ingredients. There was brown sugar, chocolate chips, fresh butter, brown eggs, marzipan, almond flour, and maple-caramel frosting. She was determined to prepare the best cake ever.

When night fell, Tooth Fairy put on her working outfit and headed to the kitchen. What she saw there was an amazing cake. Fairy Cook had outdone herself!

The Fairy Team started out with all their supplies. Soon they reached Alice's home. The fairies peeked into the window to see what was happening.

Alice was going to sleep. Actually, she wasn't.

Mom kissed her goodnight and said, "Don't worry about your tooth, Alice. We'll solve this problem tomorrow."

Alice argued, "Mom! What if it falls out while I'm sleeping? What if I swallow it?"

Mom said, "Tooth Fairy won't let that happen! She'll come as soon as it falls out and take it out of your mouth. And leave a coin," Mom smiled.

Alice whined, "I'm not sure if she exists. Why didn't she help with that awful tooth?"

Oh, no! Alice was about to lose her love of magic! The fairy team had to work really fast. They flew in silently and put the cake on the table. If Alice took three bites, the tooth would magically fall out. Fairies had brought magical cakes so many times. But still, they always felt nervous.

Fairy Cake and Tooth Fairy silently placed the cake on the table. But Fairy Cook accidentally bumped Alice's lamp. Alice turned over so fast that the fairies had to hide behind the curtain.

Alice sat up and looked at the cake. "Good try, Mom!" she said. "But I can't eat it. It's going to hurt." Tears filled her eyes. "Oh! Those rainbow balls look so yummy! And the pink whipped cream. If only I could try this cake." Alice reached towards the cake, but stopped.

Tooth Fairy understood that they had to move fast. "Come on, fairies!" she said. "Get that pillow and throw it at Alice's back."

The fairies threw the pillow as hard as they could. Alice bobbed forward - only a little - but just enough. Her finger stuck into the beautiful pink cream. She took it out and automatically licked the cream.

It was so delicious!

Alice totally forgot about her fears, wobbly tooth, and decision not to eat. She ate one lick after another with a smile.

Suddenly... what was it? She felt something hard in her mouth. She pulled out her first baby tooth.

She shrieked happily, "Mommy! It worked!"

Alice ran to her Mom and cried, "Thanks to your yummy cake, my tooth fell out! And it didn't hurt at all!"

"What cake?" Mom licked her finger and said. "I have no an idea what's going on here, but let's celebrate this big event by eating the cake together?"

Alice giggled, "I like loose teeth more and more."

"But we'll have to brush our teeth again. We don't want leftovers in our mouth for the whole night."

"No problem, Mom!" Alice agreed. "I love brushing my teeth. My toothpaste tastes almost as good as this cake." Alice started eating.

"I like this girl!" said Fairy Dentist.
"She seems very clever."

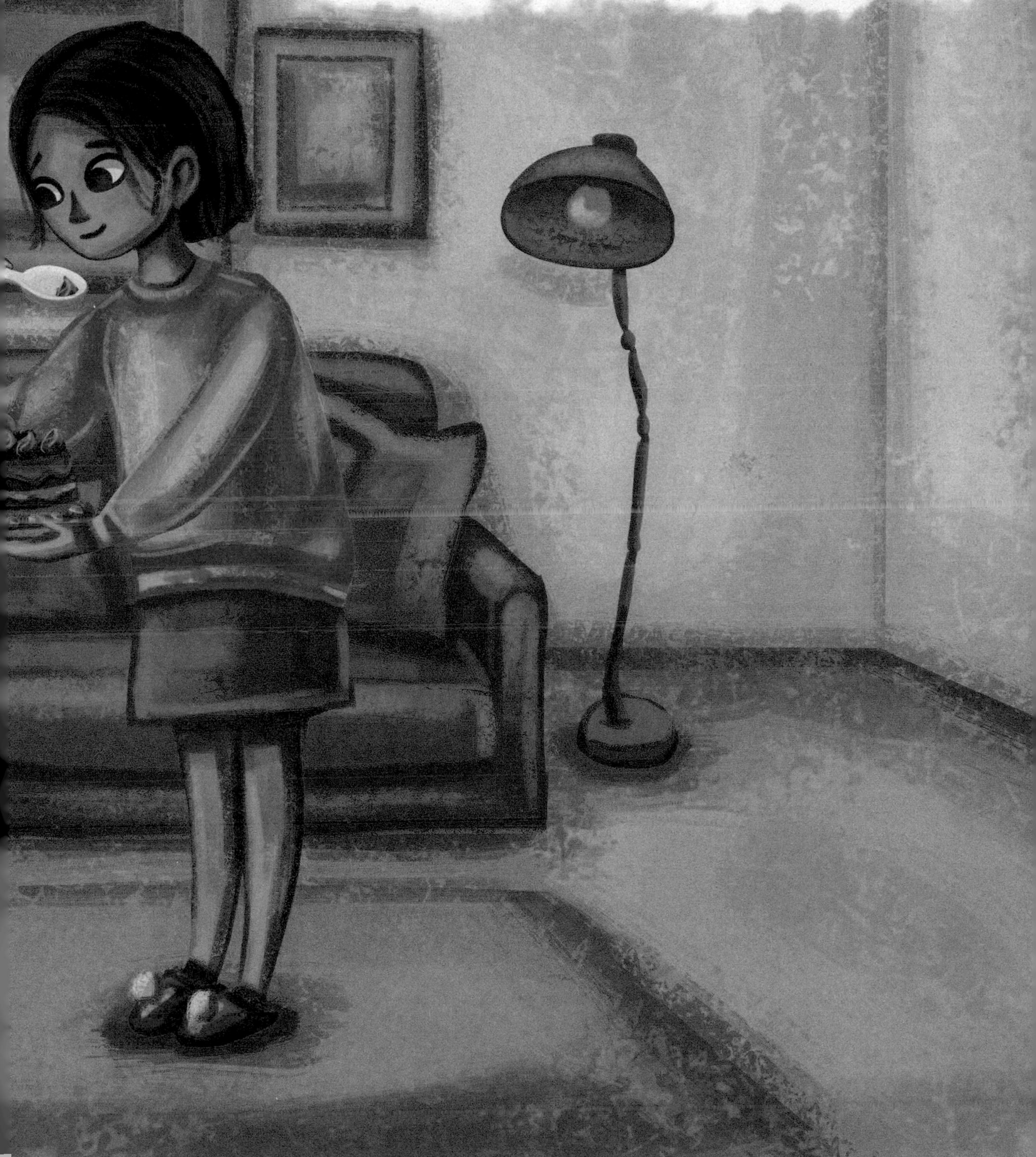

The fairies felt quite satisfied. The tooth fell out. Alice was happy, and all her fears were gone. They could rest on a tree a bit.

Smiling, Fairy Cook said, "Toothy, your powder always works! Not a single kid can resist this magic."

Tooth Fairy said, "Usually, that's true. But this time everything worked out thanks to your cooking talent."

Fairy Cook and Fairy Dentist looked at her, trying to understand what she meant.

Tooth Fairy said, "I forgot to pour my magical powder into this cake. You are the one Alice should thank for this miracle and her trust in magic."

"Oh, Toothy," said Fairy Cook with happy tears in her eyes, "I am so glad to be part of our magical team."

"A very significant part, Cookie!" said Tooth Fairy, giving her a gentle hug.

"Oh, fairies! This is so touching! I love you both so much!" said Fairy Dentist and joined that sweet hug. "But you still need to put less sugar into your cakes, Cookie."

They all started laughing.

This was a beautiful fairy night!

Made in the USA
Las Vegas, NV
28 November 2020